P9-CJZ-244

*A tiny star fell*
*to the planet of Gloom,*
*into the yard*
*of Floridius Bloom.*

*Shining so brightly*
*it pierced Gloom's gray night,*
*and Floridius thought,*
*"I must have this Light!"*

*So a wall he began*
*and he built it so tall,*
*that it captured the Light—*
*encircled it all.*

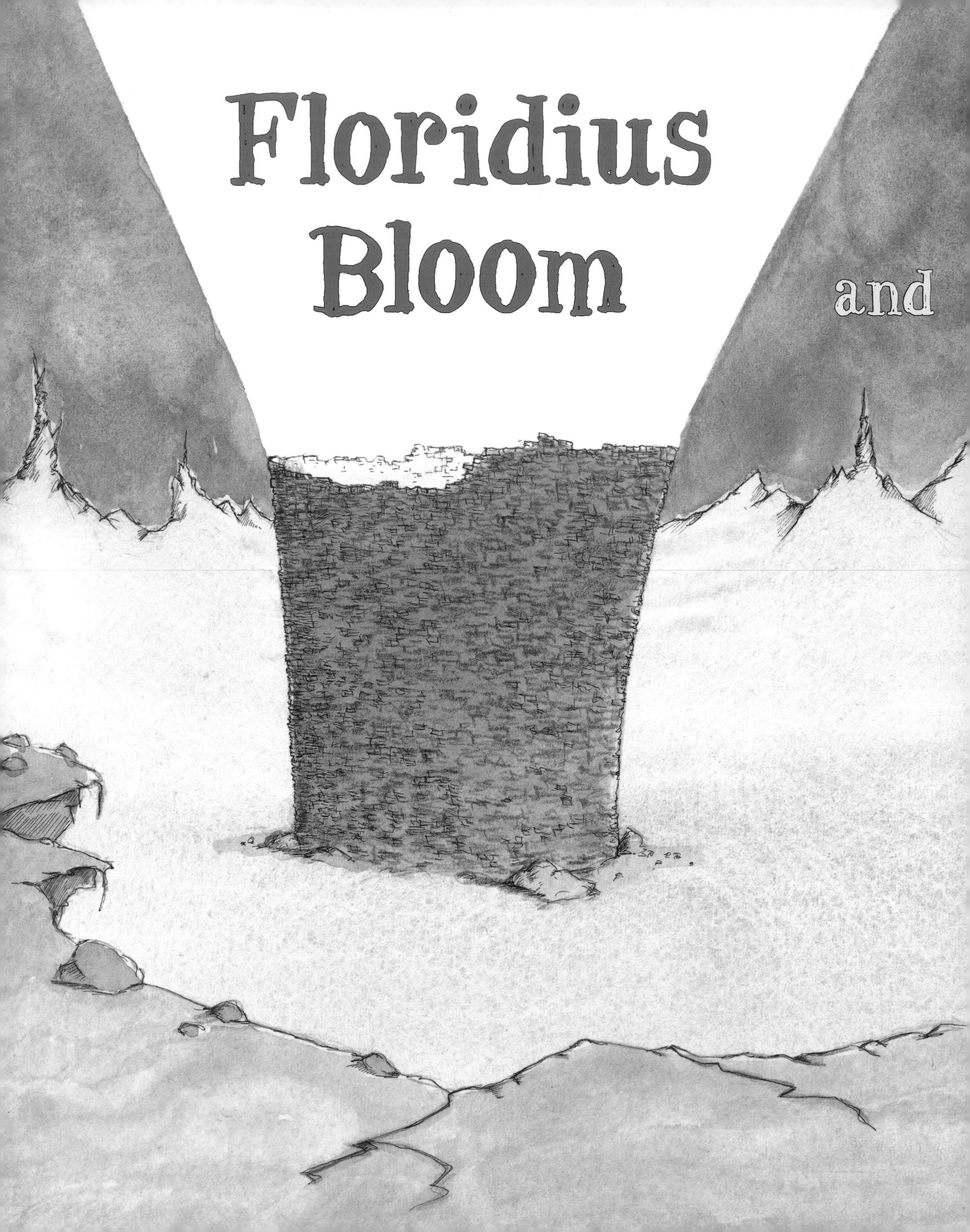
Floridius
Bloom
and

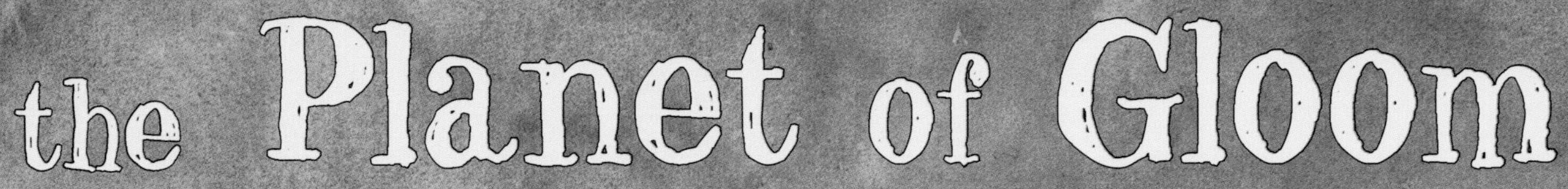


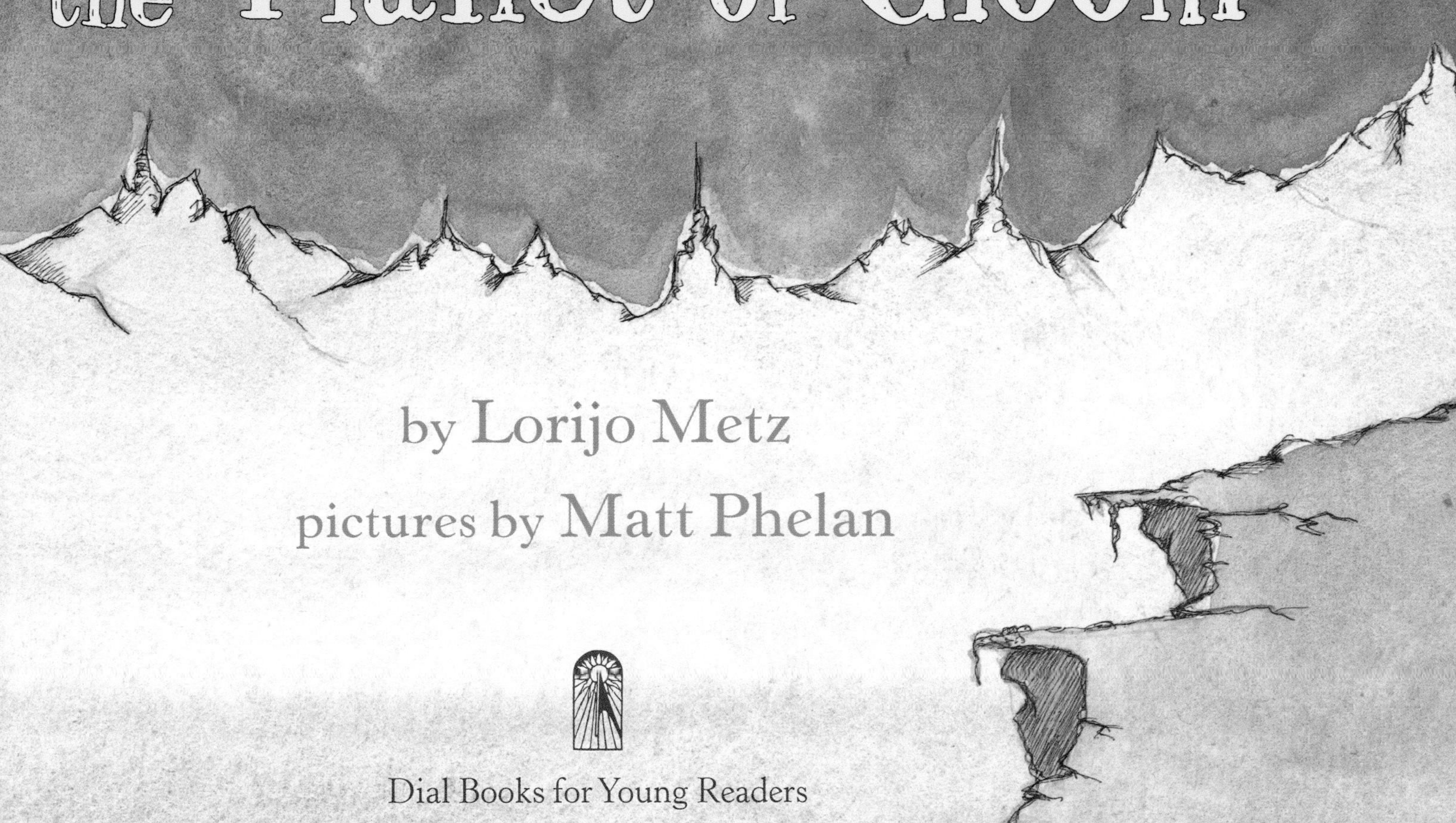

by Lorijo Metz
pictures by Matt Phelan

Dial Books for Young Readers

Floridius Bloom awoke. He shook his head and wriggled his toes. As always, the wigglyfluffs and Monsters of Gloom had invaded his dreams. "Another day, another brick," he sighed, when suddenly he heard—

Tap, tap, THUNK.

Floridius Bloom sat up.

Tap, tap, PLUNK.

"Yipes!" cried Floridius. "Those bothersome wigglyfluffs are nibbling on my prize cherriflox!" Floridius jumped out of bed and rushed to his garden.

But he saw no wigglyfluffs.

Tap, tap, CLUNK.

Floridius turned—someone had knocked some bricks out of his wall.

"Just as I've feared. The Monsters of Gloom have come to steal my Light!"

Floridius ran to the wall, picked up a brick, and was about to shove it back into place, when—

Tap, tap, WUNK.

"YE-OUCH!" shrieked Floridius.

"Sorry," squeaked a voice.

"Sorry? Sorry?!" Floridius hobbled away as four more bricks went KERPLUNK.

"Wanted a peek," said the little head attached to the voice.

"Who are you?" cried Floridius.

"Zrill," squeaked the voice, and disappeared from the opening.

"Wait! OW! You broke my toe!" Floridius hopped to the wall.

Floridius stuck his head through the hole and watched Zrill disappear into the darkness. Just when he thought there was nothing left to see . . . two bright shiny eyes stared out of the gloom.

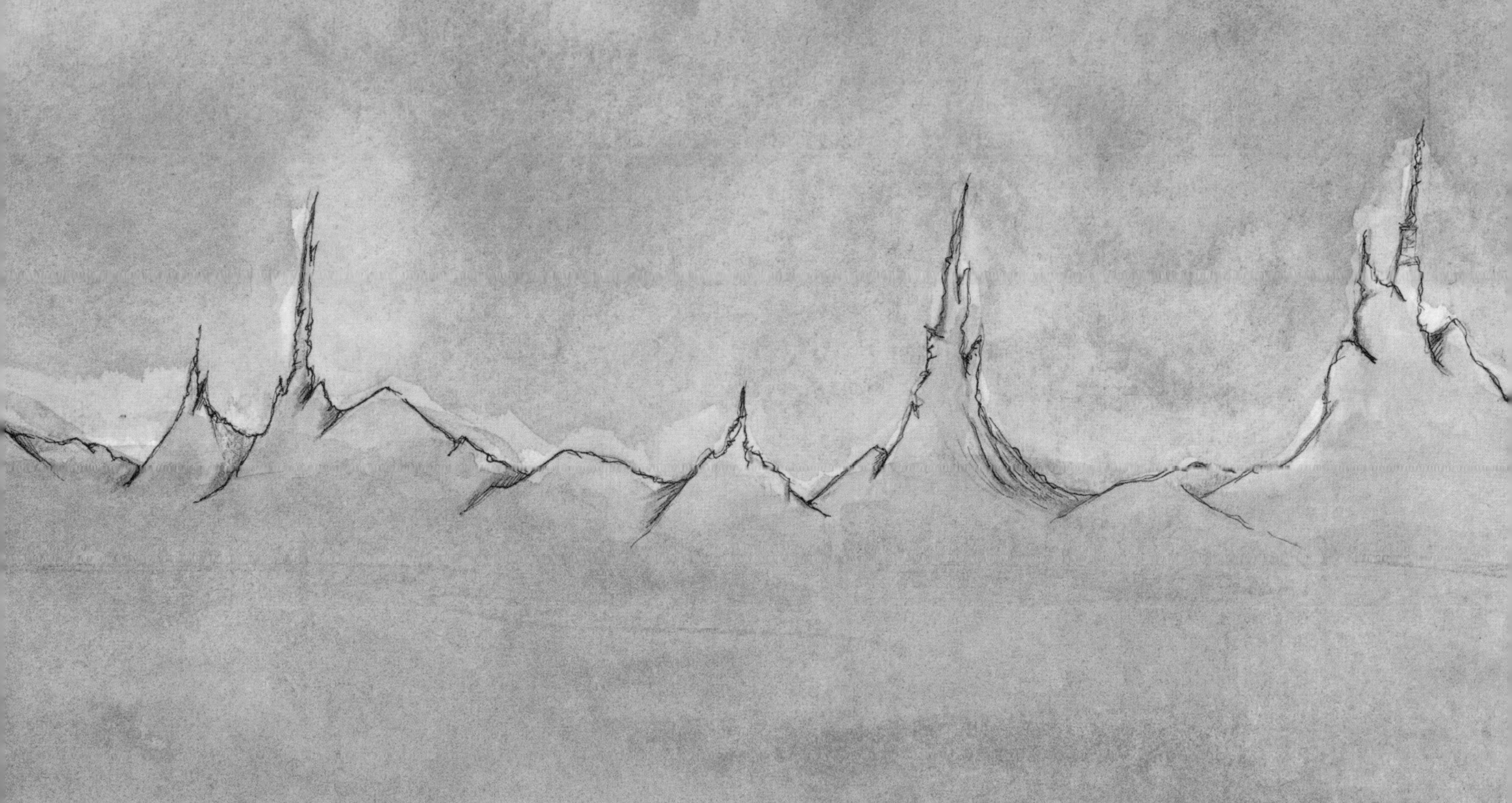

"Follow," squeaked Zrill.
And for some reason, Floridius did.

Limping after Zrill, teetering and tripping through the gray darkness of Gloom, Floridius began to see "things." Some were tall and some were small, but all had eyes that glowed.

"The Monsters!" he cried, bumping into Zrill. "You've led me straight to the Monsters!" And then it happened . . .

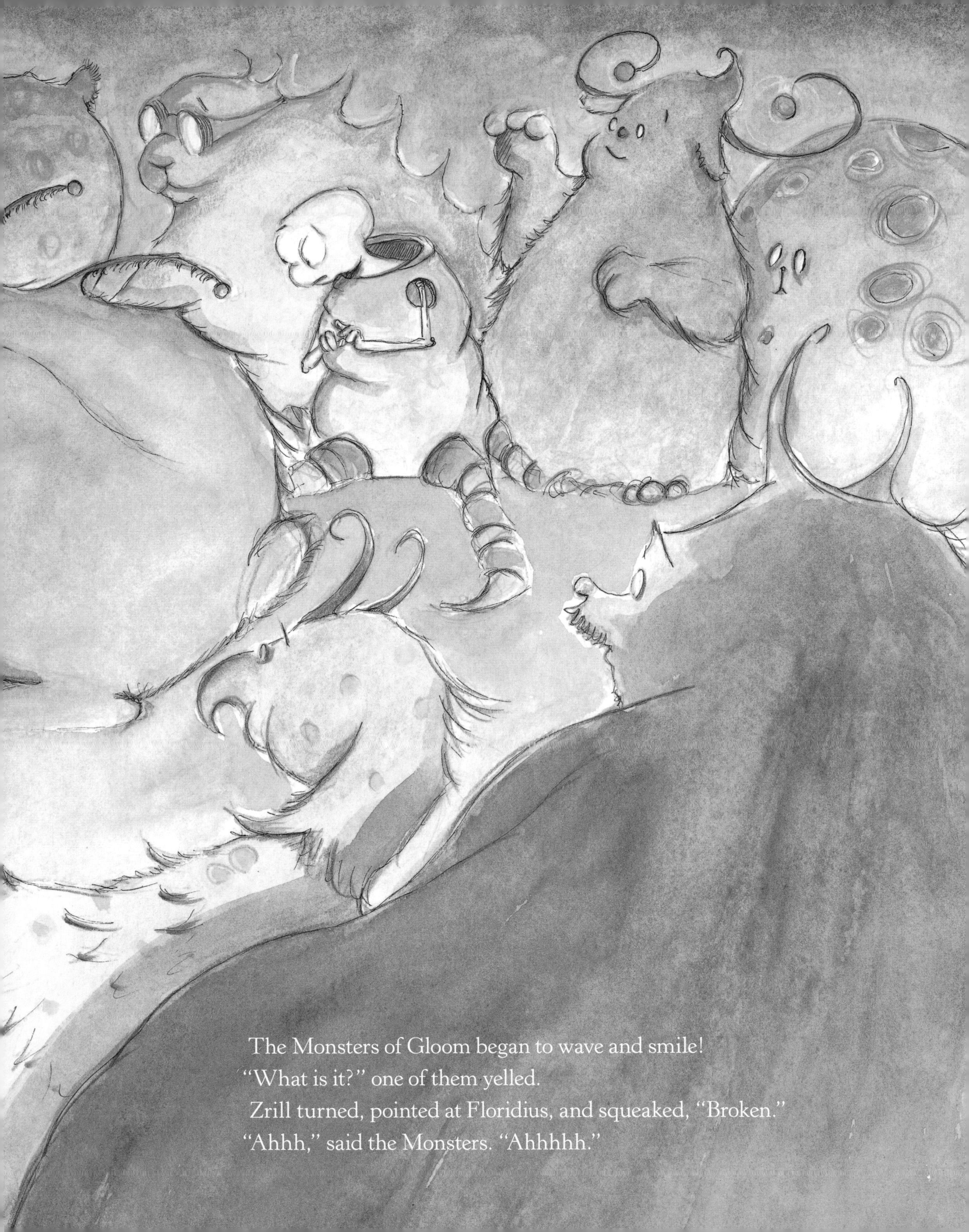

The Monsters of Gloom began to wave and smile!
"What is it?" one of them yelled.
Zrill turned, pointed at Floridius, and squeaked, "Broken."
"Ahhh," said the Monsters. "Ahhhhh."

On they traveled, farther and farther. Floridius began to notice small gray dwellings dotting the darkness. Zrill stopped and pointed at one. "Mother," he squeaked.

"Monster?" moaned Floridius.

"Mother!" squeaked Zrill, grabbing Floridius by the hand.

Inside was a creature that looked just like Zrill—only much larger.
"You're late," she said, and, "Oh my!"
Zrill pointed to Floridius's toe and squeaked, "Fix, Mother?"

Floridius remembered his toe and felt a little silly because it didn't hurt as much anymore. He looked around the room.

And for some reason, Floridius felt lonely.

Mother helped Floridius to a chair. "May I look, Mr. . . .?"
"Bloom," said Floridius.
"Ah . . . Bloom!" said Mother as Zrill hopped out of the room.

She lifted his foot and looked at his toe.
"Needs rest, Mr. Bloom . . . Someone to look after you?"
"No one," replied Floridius.
"Ahhh," said Mother, looking deep into his eyes. "Ahhhhh."

Mother propped Floridius's feet on a cushion, placed a blanket on his lap, and brought him a dish of warm gray mush.

"Better?" she asked, when suddenly Zrill popped into the room.

"Mother fixed?" he squeaked, as two more just like him popped in behind.

"Star Light," one squeaked to Floridius, "hurt?"

"Awful?" squeaked another.

"What silly notions," said Floridius. "The Light fills my home with cheezblooms and cherriflox, brickelseeds and starshines! And . . ." Floridious huffed. "I have a bench outside, for sitting and gazing upon my star whenever I please."

"And friends?" Mother asked. "Any friends, Mr. Bloom?"

"Me!" squeaked Zrill.

Floridius Bloom opened his mouth, but for once, he had nothing to say.

That night Mother brought a pile of soft covers and a warm drink. She tucked him in and trilled, "Sweet dreams, Bloom."

And, for the first time, Floridius did not dream of Monsters.

He awoke rested, but with a slight throb in his toe. "Perhaps I should stay a bit longer," he thought. Floridius closed his eyes, but this time an image appeared: not just one wigglyfluff, but hundreds of them—munching on his garden! Floridius jumped up and rushed out of the house.

Dashing madly across Gloom, back to his wall, Floridius popped his head through the opening, and stopped.

His Light, it seemed almost—too bright?

Squinching his eyes, Floridius squeezed through the hole and made his way to the garden. He groped about, picked a blossom, held it to his nose, and sniffed. "Ahhh, cheezbloom, ahhhhh!"

Then Floridius closed his eyes and heard—silence. No wigglyfluffs. No Monsters. Nothing at all. Floridius was completely alone.

Floridius walked back to the wall and stared at the hole. "I suppose I should close it up," he said. Suddenly—out of the gray gloom walked Zrill.

"Another peek?" he squeaked.

Floridius smiled.

Floridius beamed!

Zrill climbed through the hole, blinking and rubbing his eyes. Finally, he walked over to Floridius. Together, they turned and peered at the top of the wall.

"I believe my wall is complete," said Floridius. "Now what am I to do?"

"Down, down, DOWN!" squeaked Zrill, as he ran back to the wall.

"Why, yes!" Floridius laughed. "Take it ALL down, of course! Another day, another brick!"

"'Nother day," squeaked Zrill and began to climb.

"Wait, Zrill!" cried Floridius. "Where are you going?!"

But Zrill did not answer.

Tap, tap tap . . .

Floridius looked up. There was Zrill, waving from the top of the wall.

Tap, tap, THUUUUUUUUUNK!

"'NOTHER BRICK!" he squeaked, as two more bricks went, KERRRRRRRPLUNK!

"Ahhh," said Floridius Bloom. "Ahhhhh!"

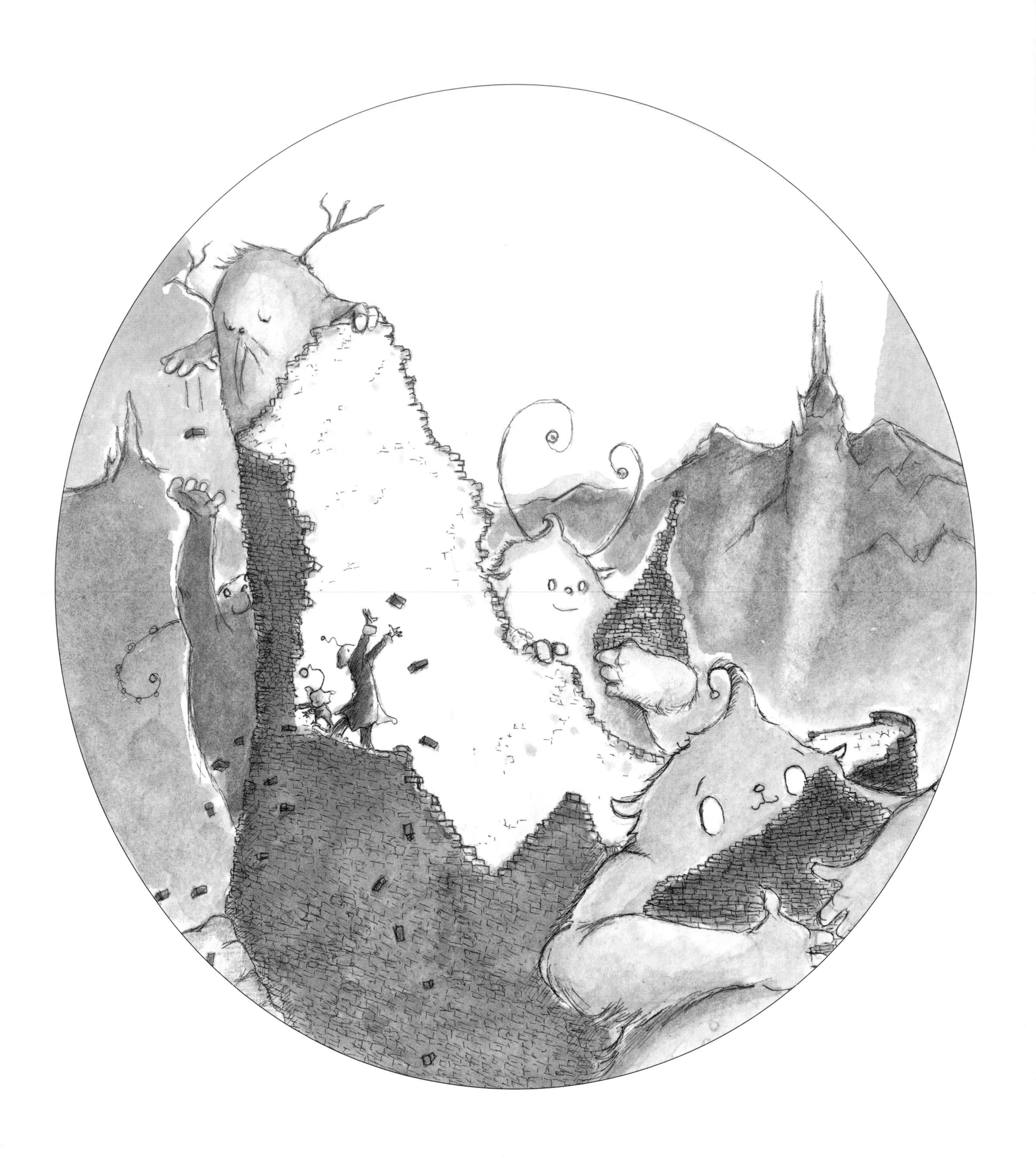

*And when the very last brick was removed from the wall,*

the little star’s Light . . .

*encircled them all.*

*To Barbara Rush, for believing in me, and Joseph Rush—you were right, there is nothing in the world like persistence!* —*LM*

DIAL BOOKS FOR YOUNG READERS
A division of Penguin Young Readers Group
Published by The Penguin Group
Penguin Group (USA) Inc., 375 Hudson Street, New York, NY 10014, U.S.A.
Penguin Group (Canada), 90 Eglinton Avenue East, Suite 700, Toronto, Ontario, Canada M4P 2Y3 (a division of Pearson Penguin Canada Inc.)
Penguin Books Ltd, 80 Strand, London WC2R 0RL, England
Penguin Ireland, 25 St. Stephen's Green, Dublin 2, Ireland (a division of Penguin Books Ltd)
Penguin Group (Australia), 250 Camberwell Road, Camberwell, Victoria 3124, Australia (a division of Pearson Australia Group Pty Ltd)
Penguin Books India Pvt Ltd, 11 Community Centre, Panchsheel Park, New Delhi - 110 017, India
Penguin Group (NZ), Cnr Airborne and Rosedale Roads, Albany, Auckland 1310, New Zealand (a division of Pearson New Zealand Ltd)
Penguin Books (South Africa) (Pty) Ltd, 24 Sturdee Avenue, Rosebank, Johannesburg 2196, South Africa
Penguin Books Ltd, Registered Offices: 80 Strand, London WC2R 0RL, England


Designed by Lily Malcom
Text set in Horlet Old Style
Manufactured in China on acid-free paper
1 3 5 7 9 10 8 6 4 2

Library of Congress Cataloging-in-Publication Data
Metz, Lorijo.
Floridius Bloom and the planet of Gloom / by Lorijo Metz ; pictures by Matt Phelan.
p. cm.
Summary: Floridius Bloom builds a high wall to keep the feared monsters of Gloom out of his light-filled garden, but one day he gets a visitor who changes everything.
ISBN 978-0-8037-3084-7
[1. Fear—Fiction. 2. Monsters—Fiction. 3. Gardens—Fiction.]
I. Phelan, Matt. II. Title.
PZ7.M56727 Flo 2007
[E]—dc22 2005004604

The illustrations were created with pencil, ink, and watercolor.